WHAT IF...?

ISBN 0-89868-434-X–Library Bound
ISBN 0-89868-435-8–Soft Bound
ISBN 0-89868-436-6-Trade

A PREDICTABLE WORD BOOK

WHAT IF...?

Story by Janie Spaht Gill, Ph.D.
Illustrations by Karen O.L. Morgan

ARO PUBLISHING

4

5

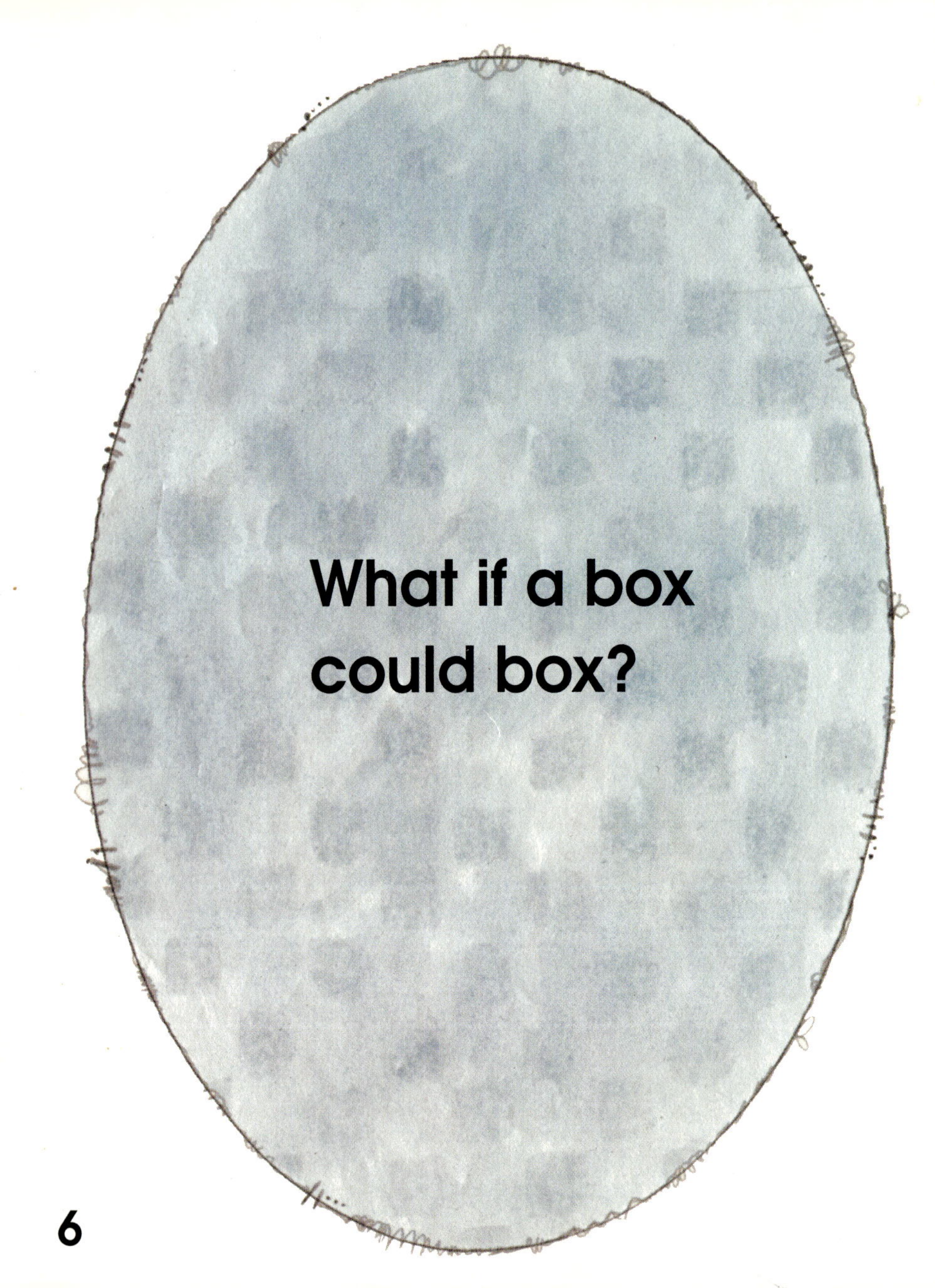

What if a box
could box?

TOP

What if a sweet roll could roll?

9

10

12

13

14

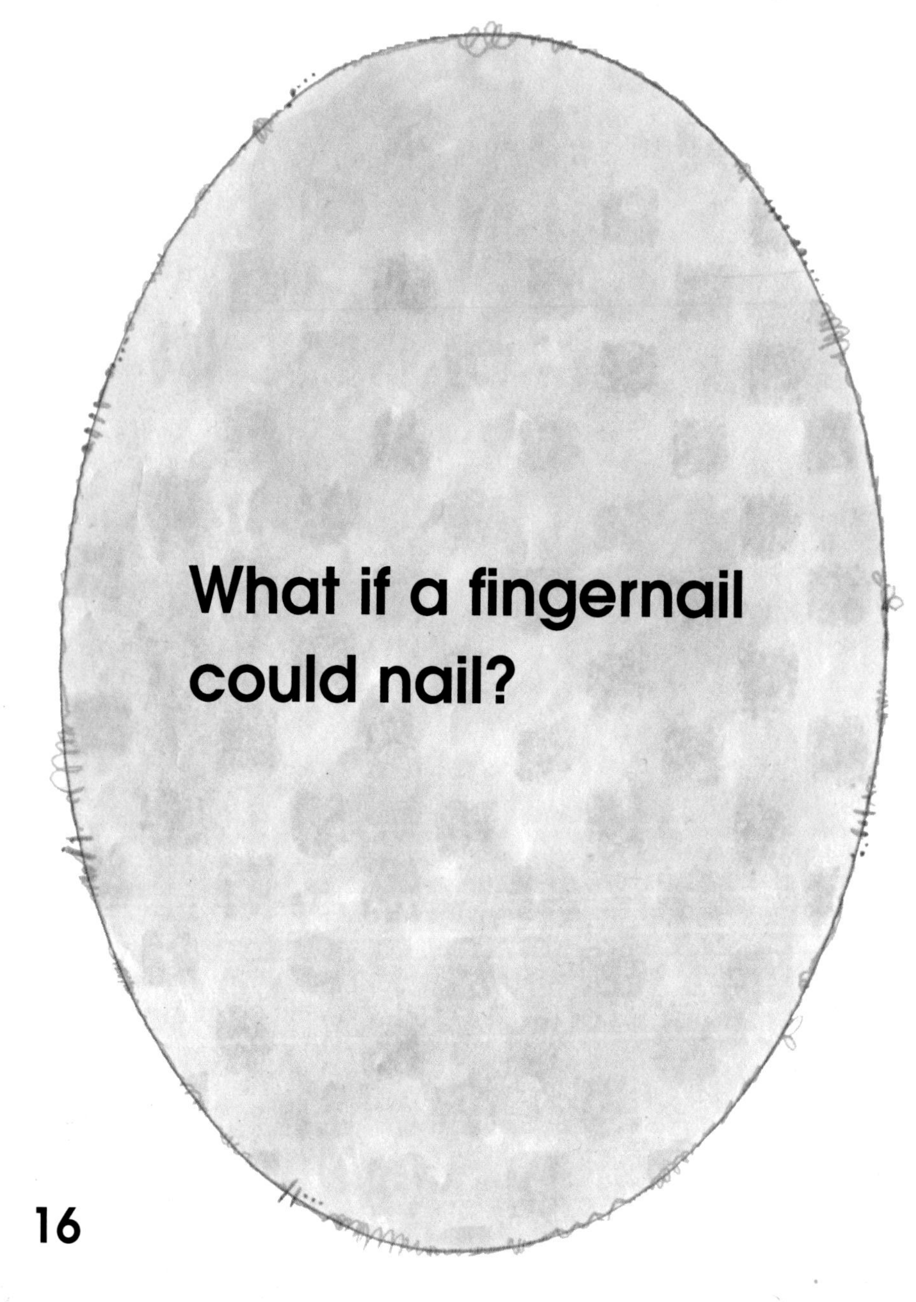
What if a fingernail
could nail?

What if a rock could
rock?

19

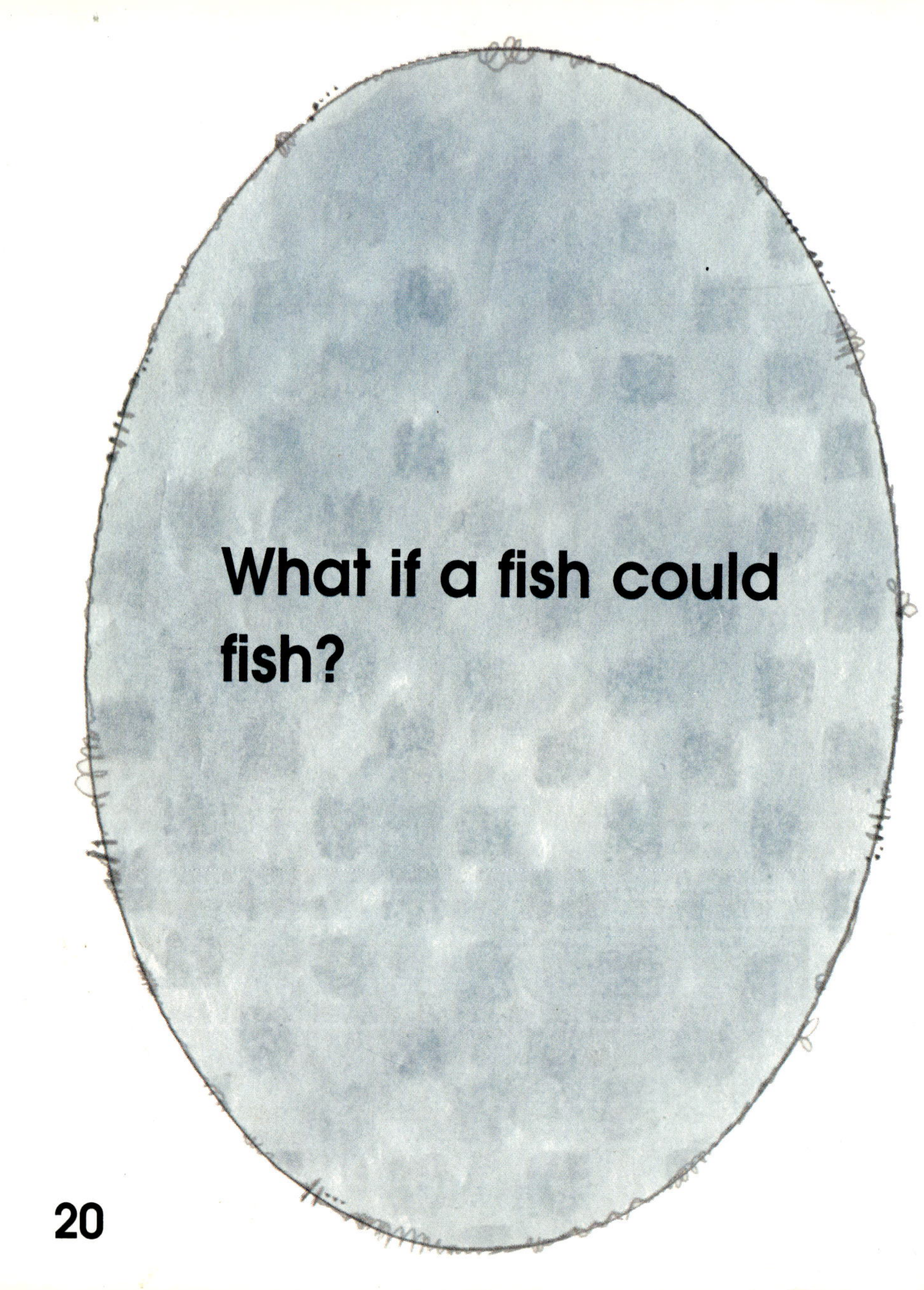
What if a fish could fish?

22

23